T0166343

How to Predict the Weather

Aaron Burch

keyhole press

Keyhole Press
an imprint of Dzanc Books
www.keyholepress.com

Portions of this book were originally published as *How to Take Yourself Apart, How to Make Yourself Anew* (PANK) and as individual short shorts in a number of journals, including *34th Parallel, Annalemma, Another Chicago Magazine, Booth, dogzplot, elimae, Everyday Genius, Kneejerk Magazine, Memorious, Monkeybicycle, Mud Luscious Press, Night Train, No Colony, Quick Fiction, Pequin, See You Next Tuesday: The Second Coming, Sleepingfish, Sir! Magazine, Storyglossia,* and *Wigleaf.*

ISBN 978-0-9821512-6-6

Cover illustration by E.B. Goodale.
www.ebgoodale.com

www.howtopredicttheweather.com

You wait, You wait
You wait for summer, then you wait for rain

—"The Wait," Built to Spill

OVERCAST

I DON'T WANT TO GO, she said.

I could just fold you up and put you in my pocket and keep you with me, he said. And he did just that, in half, then half again.

He could remember only two facts from growing up: nothing can be folded in half more than 11 times, and swallowed gum stays in your body for 7 years. He folded her in half and tucked her in. There, there.

Or, he folded as many times as he could, counting. He put her in his mouth and swallowed, pushing down his throat with index finger, inviting her to stay forever.

PREDICT THE WEATHER. *Don't tell anyone, don't share predictions or spread rumors. Don't take pride in correct guesses. Keep track, logs. Ignore forecasts, percentages, possibilities. Amass records, case histories. Avoid the impulse to diagnose. Organize the data into charts, graphs, lists. Put in alphabetical order, then numerical—small to large, reverse. Randomize. Study tide tables, ebbs and flows, the phases of the moon. Repeat everything you've learned and watched and kept track of until it comes as second nature, like multiplication tables in grade school. Repeat again, then forget it all, purge. Watch the sky. Think of nothing. Close your eyes. What do you see?*

HE SPILLED WINE ON HIS ARM, stained. It looked like a birthmark, a burn mark, but scratched it smelled like the bottom of something cheap and red. It grew, sometimes, formed cloud shapes on his arm, up his shoulder—zoo animals, states he'd never been to. Silhouettes of constellations. He met a girl who smoked, sprinkled her ash on her arms. The embers freckled her skin, became darker when she tanned, and he thought of clouds growing pregnant with rain. You don't drink wine, she said. I used to, he told her. She'd trace the outline with her fingertips, his hairs standing on end, veins tickling. They drove to parking lots and watched meteor showers from sleeping bags.

WHOA, DOG, he called. Heel.

I haven't taught him that yet, she said. I mostly just let him pull.

They'd talked about getting a dog since moving in together. Now, she had the puppy. He refused to call him anything but Dog.

She stopped. What do you think happened? she asked.

He looked up, saw a huge pile of discarded clothes and boxes and furniture. Like an entire apartment had pulled over to the side of the road after a night of drinking and vomited.

Somebody get thrown out? he said. He let go the leash and the dog ran around, sniffing from one artifact to the next.

She picked up a photo album, started flipping through. Wow. Look at these guys, she said. They look like everyone I went to high school with.

He walked over, looked at the pictures of a group of friends mugging for the camera. They were drinking from forties and a keg, giving the finger and devil horns. He started picking up clothes, holding them out in front of himself. He opened a drawer, found rows of videotapes.

The dog barked and he looked up, saw other people approaching as if they'd been waiting for someone else to come by and dig in first.

It's OK, Dog, he said. It's OK.

He walked over and grabbed the dog's leash, went back and continued looking through the videos. Most looked bought used from Blockbuster or the library, some had handwritten labels. She was still looking through the photo album, laughing and looking at each closely like she might find herself there in the background of one.

The last two videos in the back were unmarked and he thought they were probably blank, but also couldn't help wondering if they might be something else. He tucked them in his coat, then went and grabbed the dog's leash, started pulling him to the street.

C'mon, he called. Let's get before everyone else gets here. She walked over, still holding the photo album and bent down, petted the dog.

On the walk back, he kept thinking what they might be, the videos he'd grabbed. He imagined getting home and watching them together, locking the dog out of the bedroom and role-playing, making believe they were the two in the movie, watching themselves. Like she'd kicked him out and threw all his shit out in the street, yelled out the window at him as he drove away maybe, but now he'd come back and they were making up. Like the dog barking outside the bedroom door had been theirs for years and he'd been harder to leave than any of his other shit, everything piled up down at the end of the block that he no longer cared about, who might be going through it, what they might be taking.

GUT YOURSELF. Slice first from wrist to elbow fold—slow and smooth, the sharper the blade the better. Remember the filet knife you gave your dad for Father's Day when you were ten. Remember opening day every year, gutting the fish right there in the boat, letting the insides spill out into the water. Hook in your finger and scoop like that, like cleaning a fish or veining a shrimp. Invert, turn yourself inside out like a duvet, like a shirt or sock out of the dryer. Like you'd learned in youth group, bored from the sermon, to do with a Styrofoam cup: slow and careful, lest it crack and break. Spill out onto the table. A dissection. Spread out your arms, present.

SHE LIKED DRINKING in parking lots, that was his favorite thing about her. They'd go to the liquor store and buy a case of beer, or a fifth of whiskey, or a bottle of wine, or a box of wine, or sometimes even champagne, or other times a random assortment of those small, single-serving, airport-sized bottles of whatever they kept at the counter. And then go to the Walmart or the post office or a bowling alley and park and just hangout next to the trunk, or maybe pace around the lot, and they'd get drunk. She said it made her feel like she was in high school, and he knew exactly what she meant. He'd hated high school, hated all the people who loved it and missed it and pined for those days, but also kind of loved trying to recreate things he'd never created in the first place. He didn't drink in high school and had never before drank out of a cooler in his trunk, outside the automotive repair entrance of a Walmart, but he liked when they'd get back in his car and make out a nd dry hump, and maybe she'd slide her hand down his pants and jerk him off a little or she'd grab his hand and slide it under her shirt, or up her skirt, but they wouldn't go all the way because they were just teenagers, figuring it all out, though neither ever voiced that aloud. He liked it because he'd never done that the first time around, when he actually had been a teenager, and also because they didn't have to say that's what they were doing. He liked feeling like what he assumed it would have been like to be in high school love.

Some nights they'd go to this strip mall just outside of town where the main establishment was this huge Chinese buffet that they always talked about going to but never did. There was a small place around the side of the building that, on Wednesday nights, hosted Keno, and then on Fridays, Bingo. They'd drink in the parking lot and then go in and play Keno, or Bingo, depending on the night, with all these people they'd never seen anywhere else in town. He'd wonder where they'd all come from, and he liked that about it, too.

They'd go and she would always bring this little elephant pin. She'd keep it in her pocket and then as soon as everything was ready to start, she'd take it out and ask him to pin it on her, and it would feel like attaching a corsage, or at least what he'd assumed that would have felt like, if he'd gone to a dance in high school and ever attached a corsage before.

All those times, they never won anything, but it was still fun and seemed worth it. He told her once that it didn't seem like much of a good luck charm, since they'd never won anything, not once, but she just shrugged her shoulders and smiled. She didn't agree or disagree, didn't try to argue.

THE FORECAST CALLED FOR RAIN, 100% chance, but outside their window was a blue chalkboard of a sky, wiped clean. He'd never heard anything predicted with such certainty; he thought how he'd looked outside at downpours while listening to reports of the *likelihood* of rain, the *possibility*. It looked, felt, like the first or last days of a long summer. The beginning or end.

They'd had a picnic planned, but cancelled. He watched out the window, unsure what to hope for. Unsure what outcome was the underdog, whether to root for or against.

He pulled the blinds, got in his car, drove. He wanted the expanse of sky to open up above him like the road below. Wanted to find that moment the weather changed, where forever finally ended. He drove, forgot what he was looking for.

WHERE ARE WE GOING, he asked.

We're driving, she said.

He thought about that, nodded.

Weeks, they'd been driving. Maybe more. Maybe much more. He'd lost track of time, had no idea how long they'd been on the road.

At night, they slept in the car, or they found a campsite and slept on the ground. They didn't have a tent or sleeping bags or a tarp or blanket. They kept one another warm with their bodies, woke in the morning sore and wet with dew. They'd shake, to dry off like a dog and also in attempt at some kind of body realignment. It didn't seem to work on either account but, still, the action continued.

He preferred the nights in the car but thought he was supposed to prefer the great outdoors—the sight of stars overhead, the getting back to nature, the *aliveness* in the air, and being next to one another instead of the barrier of armrests and emergency break.

I don't think I like not knowing where we're going, he said.

He'd assumed she'd lost track of time as well, but never asked. He could barely remember where they'd started, but couldn't ask after that either.

Is that a double negative, she said. She didn't look at him, like there was something outside that she was trying to figure out.

I don't not think so, he said, trying to be funny. She still didn't look at him, and didn't say anything in reply either.

Outside, through the windshield but in the direction through her window, clouds had moved in, were growing dark. He smiled.

BE PURE. *Be Icarus and Dionysus both. Look into the face of others and ask—with your wings and with your eyes—for their pain. And when they offer up their suffering, their sorrow and grief, heartache and sadness, take it all into your mouth, your beak, and hold tight but careful like a stork carrying a baby. Bundle it all together and carry it away, up toward the sun, continuing toward the heat with a pureness of heart. Let it overtake you, let the sun burn the gift you've brought. Let it burn you as well, if it must. Sacrifice.*

HE WALKED IN HIS HOUSE, threw his keys on the table next to the small ivory elephant, and stopped.

He was calm, careful not to yell.

What? his roommate asked. His roommate because he'd needed a place and this was what he found. Needed a place when moving back to town, after following a couple of different girls to various places across the country. Places he never thought he'd drive through much less live. Cities like Akron, Ohio; Tallahassee, Florida. Some days it seemed weirder than others to hang out on the couch and watch TV and share dinner with someone he didn't really know, but it worked well enough.

When he didn't respond, the roommate gave a little head nod and asked What? again. Then he scratched his chest and said, Oh, right. These. He was wearing suspenders and he slipped a thumb under each strap and gave them a flick against his chest. Thought I'd mix it up, try them out, the roommate said.

He thought of his own suspenders, stashed in a box in the back of his closet. The suspenders she bought from a thrift store as a joke. And how, one night, he drunkenly put them on, even though he'd already taken his shirt off. Yes, she'd laughed, and yes her laughter turned him on as much as it always did. And then, a few nights later, drunk again, *she* put them on topless. She worked them so the straps were perfectly balanced over her which, yes, was incredibly sexy, and when they slipped, the straps just pushed her together which, yes, both hilarious and sexy. And he thought how, when a girl like that asks you to move to middle of nowhere, Nebraska, which is basically anywhere in Nebraska, you nod your head and say yes, of course, and then when you get there and she leaves you, you wander around aimlessly for a while, and find another girl or two to follow to new cities and you keep the suspenders in a box with everything else you should throw away but you just can't make yourself, until one day, you come home and find your roommate in suspenders and it ruins every image you've tried to hold onto, even when you were mostly trying not to.

REMEMBER THE MYTH *of looking directly into the sun. The milk cartons cut into a makeshift periscope. Remember your brothers and sisters having to turn away, their eyes too weak. Forget their fall, the push, the fact that that was the last time you saw them. Look up to the sun and ask if your strength is a gift or a curse. Push up, out of your nest, and fly toward it, past the caladrius, feeling for a brief moment a kinship you've missed, you've thought was gone, you've thought wasn't possible. Feel the heat burn away your outer layer, as if a film had built up over time and you hadn't even noticed, then tuck and fall. Plummet. Past the caladrius again, past others trying to follow its ascent, and crash into the water. Feel new, cleansed, reborn.*

HOME ALONE, he went straight for the kitchen. Straight like an accident, on purpose, like he didn't know where he was going but couldn't wait until she'd left. She'd run to the bank, or the grocery store, or he-don't-know-where because he wasn't really listening when she'd called to him on her way out the door. He pulled out the receipt, held it in front of his face, made himself look at it.

The first time he found it—tucked away, near the back of a drawer they rarely used—he'd been looking for the scissors, or some Post-Its, or a battery, or this receipt. Then he started getting it whenever home alone. He studied it, the numbers—the price, the barcode, the date and time. They didn't mean anything, save for being the same numbers he always found, but that first time, he'd looked at a calendar, done the math. He'd figured it out.

He pictured the different scenarios for what might have happened to the shirt from the receipt, why he'd never seen it. Pictured what it might have looked like, how she'd look in it. It could be hidden, he thought— from herself, so as to not be reminded; or from him, so as to not make him ask questions; or from everyone, the whole world, so as to not have to share the memory, the specialness of it, every time she wore it. It could be in a special box somewhere, along with God-knows-what-else, he couldn't bear to imagine. She might have lost it, or thrown it away, or given it to Goodwill, or burned it in some kind of ritual of cleansing and moving on. She might have returned it. Except he was holding the receipt, so she couldn't have taken it back. And he couldn't picture her getting rid of it or cleansing or moving on.

A noise outside and he stood straight and rehearsed—*I was just looking for the scissors*; or: *Post-Its*; or: *a battery*; or: *this*, holding it up—but it was only a car driving by.

In high school, he'd taught himself how to fold paper cranes, his girlfriend's favorite. He spent a weekend making them, one after another, using every piece of paper he could find, all weekend. Early Monday morning, he filled her locker with them, barely able to wait for her to open the door, for the cranes to spill out everywhere. He hadn't folded another since that weekend but, without thinking about it, he was twirling the receipt in his fingers, folding, in half, into triangles, little waves of folds. He pulled at the head and tail and the body pillowed out like taking in a deep breath. He held it in his pushed-together palms, then held them out the open window and released. He imagined himself a magician letting go the dove after having made it appear out of his hat or from behind a tissue, and the dove, the crane, flapped its wings, glided out over the audience and away.

WATCH THE CALADRIUS give itself to the sun, watch the eagle's fall and rebirth. Remember the story of Abraham, the test, but forget the last minute reprieve. Watch the other birds, the mother's chewing the food first and then feeding it to their young. Compile all this watched and learned knowledge, feel it pulse down from your brain to your heart, feel it coursing through your veins. Don't think, don't stop and consider, don't try to do the math. It adds up: the killing, the feeding, the rebirth. Count to three. Spread your wings out to your side in full span. Give of yourself.

HE LOOKED AT THE ROWS of monitors, saw her flight was delayed due to weather. Outside, through the glass, motion-sensored doors, he didn't think it looked so bad.

He sat down, waited, thought about maps. How, when a flight is shown from one city to another, its path is nearly always in an arc—a curve of movement, departure and arrival. Something about the shortest distance between two points being a straight line, and the variable of time, delays. Hopefully, he thought, the clouds will clear and you'll be here soon. I'll try to think of an example, an explanation; something to tell you. I'll tell you all about it.

SHE BALANCED HERSELF above him, floating in the air, and he thought of clouds, of always wishing he could reach up and touch them. She hovered atop a mattress of air, like that skateboard in the *Back to the Future* movie, like two magnets, like a hovercraft. He propped himself on elbows, arched his back, tried to lean up and into her but only pushed her further away. She'd been working on the trick for months, years, trying to get it just right. Turn it off, he said. Can you turn it off. He reached up to grab her and her body started turning, rotating out and away.

HE OPENED THE CUPBOARD, asked, Which cereal is the best?

I don't want to waste my time, he said. Hook me up, no fooling around.

He'd woken on the bottom of a bunk bed, wrapped in scratchy Spiderman sheets and a camouflage blanket. For the first time in his life, he'd thought about the benefits of thread count, wondered at what age the minutiae of comfort started being so important.

Two kids were watching TV, bouncing on couches, and playing with toys. They ran over to help.

These are for grownups, they said. And these are for kids. They separated the two groups, parting the cupboard like Moses or an adult pulling apart fighting children.

He'd coughed when going to put on his clothes, heavy with leftover smoke, so was standing in the kitchen in only boxers. The linoleum was cold and a little sticky.

These are the grownup ones? he asked.

Yes. Grownups, the boy said. Kids, he said, pointing.

Grownups! Kids! The girl echoed.

He looked at both groups, realized they hadn't really answered his question. He hadn't had a bowl of cereal in years, maybe since his own chicldhood. She didn't eat breakfast, didn't like milk.

I think I want one with cartoons on the box, he said. What's the best one with cartoons on the box?

Cartoons? Cartoons! they both said. One by one, they pulled the boxes out of the cupboard, put them back in, looking for the perfect box. He looked around, surveyed the house, listened for any stirring.

WHEN STUCK, *lost, confused, frustrated: do as before. Don't fear repetition. This can be used for other moments; use when needed. Use carbon paper, stencils, mirrors, projectors. Don't forget the tools available to you. In fact, you may want to make note of these now for later, while you are thinking about them. Writing commits to memory and, when unsure, revert to rote.*

THEY GOT OUT OF BED and peeked through the slats of blinds. Every morning this was their routine, the first thing they did: looked outside, searching for sun. And every morning, every morning for longer than they could remember, saw only clouds. Before, there were mountains looking back, climbing up out of the earth; nights of stars, constellations and meteors. Those images, they had them stored with blurry edges and a lack for specifics. They remembered being told to never look directly at the sun, that it would make you blind, but it was beginning to feel like they could maybe use a little blindness.

And then, of course, as all streaks end, as nothing is forever, as every cloud has a silver lining, they looked out the window one morning and there it was, between the silver-lined clouds. A part in the sky like someone had sliced it open, had pulled apart the clouds like the blinds they were looking through. They stared at that sky, at each other. He wanted to get in his car and drive, drive and find the ground beneath the opened sky, but then worried he wouldn't know what to do once there. They got back in bed, pulled the covers over their heads, and waited for the sky to close back up.

I HAVE STRIPES, she said, and he thought he'd misheard her.

Stripes, she said again.

What, like a cheetah, he asked.

No, she said. Cheetahs have spots. I think you mean, like a tiger. Zebra, maybe.

So, like a tiger?

No, she said again. And she looked at him, a look he wasn't familiar with. He wasn't sure what that look meant.

I can't really explain, she said. I just wanted to say something. To warn you, or whatever. And she started to undress. She took off her jacket, unbuttoned and dropped her men's tuxedo shirt, slung her bra. She kicked off her shoes, unzipped and stepped out of her skirt. Peeled off her leggings, tossed her underwear. She stood in front of him and she looked at him. He knew what that look meant. *See?*

But he still didn't see. He didn't see any stripes, he didn't know what she could have meant. All he saw was her standing there—naked, eyes closed, clothes piled around her and thrown to the side, arms outstretched like in presentation, like a statue, like some kind of religious or spiritual being. He still didn't see what she could have meant, but he nodded. When she opened her eyes, their looks met and she knew what his meant. He got it. Yes, yes, I see exactly what you meant.

INDEPENDENCE DAYS with friends, lying on the tarmac of a Walmart parking lot, she watched fireworks shoot and crackle around them.

In the mountains with family, curled in sleeping bags in a visitor center parking lot, he watched the meteor shower overhead, stars dying and fading into nothing.

Together, splayed out in driveway, silent, houselights turned off, they could barely recognize from behind the clouds each other exploding across the sky.

RUN AWAY. Have a shotgun wedding because your father never took you hunting. Because you like the sound of it, the way she wraps it around itself when she says it. Because you went camping and hiking and threw lure and line into rivers and lakes but you always knew, even then, that cleaning a fish isn't the same as pushing a knife into a deer, cutting from neck to ass. Now, realize that maybe it is. Maybe shooting beer cans off a fence is, in essence, the same as sitting in the upper deck, sharing binoculars. Stop waiting for someone to take you, tell you, show you how. Pull.

THEIR FIRST, and most recurring, date was a baseball game. She'd never before been, and he couldn't believe it. Sometimes, games and games later, she'd still slip, ask how many points they'd scored.

Not points, he'd say. Runs.

I say points.

Well, you're wrong.

Same thing. Runs. Points. You know what I mean.

Fine, he'd say. Whatever. But you're wrong. You sound like a girl.

I am a girl.

You sound like you don't know what you are talking about.

He started keeping track, the way things had changed— cloudless vs. overcast skies, explicit mentions vs. noted absences. Made silent bets with himself on the day's score, kept notebooks full of scratched counts—one, two, three, four, diagonal—looking like a prisoner counting days, a child keeping track of tic-tac-toe wins.

Once, he tried teaching her how to keep score, tracking every hit, run, out. She liked when he talked like he was teaching something.

Why? she asked.

It keeps you involved, he said. Makes you pay attention to the game, every at bat, so you don't miss anything.

Every single, little thing isn't really important overall though. I like to walk around, watch people.

It's what people used to do, he said. Before scoreboards, before televised replays. Pretty much no one does it anymore, but it can be kind of fun.

Her patience exhausted in late innings, she gave up. He pushed on, trying to prove something. At this point, anything.

WRITE IT DOWN then ball up the piece of paper, push it into your mouth. Acknowledge that it feels better in there than it did in front of your eyes. Take your time, chew slowly, savor. Think of magpies, italicize the word in your head. Magpies. Think of both the bird and the image of pie that your mind wants to draw. Swallow. If that doesn't work, go outside, sit Indian style, and draw pictures in the ground of what you wrote down. Cup the dirt into your mouth, thinking of your hands as ladles, the earth as necessity. Ladle: a vessel for transporting liquid; to transfer from one receptacle to another. If, when trying to swallow, you cough and have to spit back up some of the dirt, think of the crumbs of earth as small birds taking flight, transferring from one vessel to the next. Think of it like giving birth to an avian beginning.

LOOKS LIKE RAIN, she said, and shrugged her shoulders.

This had become her default action, this shrug, this.

He wanted to say something but didn't, wondered if she noticed the desire, the hesitation. This is what their conversations had matured into. From agreement to persuasion, apologies to resignation, stated and accepted constants. Their conversations, but mostly their arguments. This.

He thought of his dad, how, growing up, they'd been rod and reel men. Weekdays, fighting off morning and school, he was a kid; but on weekends, waking without complaint before sunrise to don waders and long underwear, he became a man. They were buddies, partners, teammates. They were fishermen. Rivers and lakes, bait and tackle, rain or shine.

Last time he was home, he was hurt to find his dad had taken up fly-fishing. It was like he'd been traded for someone else, like finding out he'd been diagnosed with something but hadn't shared the news. His old rod and reel was in the garage, hadn't been used since he-couldn't-remember-when.

Clouds don't mean rain, he said. It might clear up.

He watched her, waiting for her to shrug or agree or disagree, something. Something more than this.

WHAT DID I JUST SAY, she asked.

He'd been busying himself recreating the above cloudscapes on his arm. He rotated it toward her, pointed. But it looked backwards. Backwards and upside down. Jumbled and mangled.

That looks jumbled and mangled, she said.

I was trying, he said. The replication, he said.

You speak in too many ellipses, she said.

What do you mean? I pause too much?

No, she said. No. That's not what I said.

THEY HAD TO CALL—*he* had to call—a repairman, because when they would try to start the dryer, it made a noise like a vacuum sucking up a broken stereo. Like a dryer that needed a repairman.

He'd barely closed the front door behind him when the repairman said he found the problem. A sock sucked up into the vent. It's fixed. Just like that. He'd known the screen to the vent was missing a screw, had been putting off going to the hardware store.

His dad, he thought, would have taken the dryer apart himself, would have found the problem, fixed it. He would have gone to the hardware store and there never would have been a problem to fix. He thought of the coffee tins full of screws and nails, washers and nuts and bolts, all sizes, in the garage when he was little. His dad wouldn't have had to go to the hardware store at all. He didn't know if he had a single extra nail or screw in the house, and he didn't drink coffee.

REMEMBER AS MANY dreams from your childhood as you can. From as young as possible. Write them down—on scraps of paper, receipts, the newspaper, the palm of your hand. Sign your name like you would on the cast of your best friend's broken arm. Write them everywhere, read them back to yourself, reread. Repeat. Push them into yourself like injecting with a needle, until the dreams return, scene by scene. There.

THEY LAID OUT IN HIS YARD, watched the clouds pass overhead. Talked, shared silences, one as natural as the other. The sky smoothed clear for a moment, and they went inside. Made margaritas, took frozen glasses to the roof of the garage, watched the clouds return. They pointed and shared found shapes. A plane flew past and he wished on its contrails, like a shooting star, for the sun to never set.

The excitement of similar and individual visions in their blotted sky became their special date, their ritual. The, ritual became routine; routine, a chore. The clouds had the final say.

SHE'D BEEN GONE only a week. It may have been longer. A year? She had always been the keeper of time. He had no real way of knowing how long it had been, least not without asking her, which he couldn't.

He also could not remember how or why she'd left. Because of him? Her? He resigned himself to not knowing, sure he couldn't ask her that either.

I brought something, she said.

He looked at her, like, Oh?

Can I come in, she asked.

He looked at her again, this time, like, sure, yes, of course.

She walked in and through the house and then out into the back. He followed, a few steps behind. When he'd caught up, she held her hands out to him, together, palms up. Like being held under running water or cupping something delicate. The pose reminded him of a painting, he thought, though he couldn't picture one specifically. Inside her hands was a pile of plastic stars, like those that stick to ceilings and glow at night.

What we'll do, she said, is plant them. Water them. Let them grow, like in a garden. And when they've blossomed and are full-grown, we can release them into the sky on cloud-filled nights. So then, any night we want, we will be able to see a sky full of stars.

She said it like it was all so simple.

What about during the day, he asked.

She thought about it like she hadn't before. Then said, I couldn't think of what to plant and grow for that.

Her enthusiasm was fading and he was happy that his realism was winning, but also sad to see the fade.

Water! she said then, suddenly. We'll plant a lake or river underground and grow the blue sky itself, not the sun!

Again, it all sounded so simple.

And then he thought of the answer he'd been told to that children's question of sky's color and what makes it so. A reflection of all the water on our planet, someone had once told him. His father? A teacher? A fellow child, making it up, only to become something he still believed all these years later?

What he wanted to say to her then was: Isn't this what got us here in the first place? How, when they'd found those tufts of cloud, they'd put them in her memory box, because they didn't know what else to do with them. Until, one day, they took them out and buried them in the backyard, like a time capsule, meant only to be a shared funny moment and story. But they'd grown, overlarge and too big for the ground, like produce for a fair competition, until finally releasing themselves into the sky like hot air balloons with their ties finally cut. They'd floated up into the sky and settled in, clouding over their every day. And why had they never wondered how or where those first found seeds of cloud had come to be found by them?

DRAW DIAGRAMS OF EXPLANATION. Use detail, be intricate; don't let uncertainty excuse lack of specificity. Once complete, destroy, dismantle, etc. Erase, rip, cut, break it into pieces. Copy each small piece onto your body—cover hands, feet, arms, legs. A complete transfer, put the whole back together. Tie yourself in knots. Use folds, ripples, waves of yourself crashing into each other. Think of it, of yourself, as a complicated math equation: without one small detail, the formula doesn't work. The sum adds up to the whole, or nothing.

MY HANDS are turning into birds, she said, and he said, Really? Birds? Can't you be a little more original?

She looked at him then down at each hand, fingers and thumb pulled together into a beak.

You just want me to describe you as bird-like, he said. She smiled, and he smiled back. He liked the sound of the word, the feel of it dropping out of his mouth as he'd said it. What he didn't say was that he would have been less hesitant to describe her as more like an alpaca; or a burro, maybe. For some reason, she brought to mind ideas of fur more than feathers.

Do you know how to fold origami birds? she asked. She was sitting at the dining room table, clumsily folding a piece of paper into nothing that resembled origami.

Paper cranes? he asked.

Yeah. Those. She looked at her hands then the piece of paper, then back at her hands like they'd show her how.

No, he said. I used to but I'm sure I wouldn't be able to remember now.

Help, she said, asking and not, and looking at him with those eyes that always suckered him into everything.

I'll tell you what. Let's go to the bookstore and get a book or two and we can learn how together, I said. But can we make something else? Cranes are so obvious and basic; they're what everyone always makes. Let's be more creative.

I really only want to make birds, she said. She clawed her hands into pincers and pecked at one with the other. My hands want to make little birds.

She wrapped one hand then the other in bandages, kept them wrapped for weeks.

They want to fly but can't, she explained when he asked why. She got teary-eyed and left the room and he thought, This is getting ridiculous. He sat at the table and distracted himself with the origami books they'd bought. Made frogs and insects and dinosaurs, never folding the same thing more than once.

He walked in the front door and noticed a feather or two on the floor. Then more, everywhere, lining the hall and scattered like a cat had carried a bird into the apartment and played with it, chasing and swatting, until it finally escaped.

He called to her with exclamations in his voice. With question marks.

He found her at the table, looking sad, and

something seemed odd though it didn't immediately register. She looked at him, remained quiet. She's in shock, he thought. Then: I'm in shock. Both her hands were bandaged like they had been, though one seemed shorter. Then he noticed: the handsaw on the table, the burnt-brick darkness of the one bandage, the fact that it was bandaging a hand that was no longer there.

Please, she said. You. Help. I didn't think ahead, how I'd do one after the other. She looked at him with those eyes and he decided to keep himself there, to grab hold the shock he was in and not let go.

He picked up the saw and thought of helping his dad with small building projects when growing up. How, when cutting something, that first cut was the most important. Pull—steady and with a good force—in one long, full-blade motion and everything after comes naturally. Once the path is made, and if you keep a good, consistent rhythm, everything is easy. He plucked the teeth of the blade with his thumb then placed the end nearest the handle on her wrist, held it at a good angle, and took a deep breath.

HE LET GO HER HAND so he could stare up into the sky, tetherless. I love watching the clouds herd over the buildings, he said. If the clouds are moving fast enough, it looks like the buildings are falling, coming down on top of us.

He thought of how she was always talking about perception and perspectives—how, if you hold your eyes on one point, you could measure the speed of everything else. Or vice versa. How everything can be relative.

When he was little, the first time in the city, his uncle pointed up into the sky, called the buildings cloud-scrapers. He'd pictured scoops of ice cream, thought of the buildings later when out for family dessert. His uncle had said he had a tides table for the clouds, always knew when they'd be high or low, ebbing or flowing.

He watched the buildings fall toward them a little longer then looked down, around, and she wasn't there. She didn't realize he'd stopped, didn't stop together. A woman he'd assumed was her looked up into the sky beside and with him. The woman-that-wasn't-her looked at him, smiled, agreed.

HOLD THE LEASH TAUT. Not tight. There is a difference, admittedly subtle. Beyond semantics, though also in the way you hold your mouth open: like going to the doctor, or singing. What matters most is what you picture when you hear the word slack—cursive handwriting? Loops and figure eights? Is it one long, unbroken line like drawn without picking up pen from paper, no sharp corners? You may have it. Everything else comes naturally, builds like all by itself. Hold your arm out, not too straight. Flex, but don't tighten your muscles.

CREEPING, ducking, peeking—her birthmark had seemed to always be in motion; coming up out of shirts, flying under chin and ear, across her face. He loved that mark, loved watching it dance across her until, overwhelmed, he began fearing it was all he loved. Later, he could never fully recall why he'd left her. He spilled a bottle of Merlot on his leg to recreate, to commemorate, and it dried the color of salmon, freshly grilled. He'd always thought the mark was the color of wine. He tried again, a bottle of Cabernet, more expensive, but found the same result: salmon, possibly grilled over mesquite.

She had a twin, technically more beautiful. Her skin, her entire body he had assumed, was shiny clear, birthmarkless. Sometimes, he felt sad for her, to have missed out on such a beautiful gift, to be taunted by it every time she looked at her twin.

He moved to Wisconsin, the state he thought most resembled the mark on her neck. Nights, he drove to bars, asked if they'd seen a girl, beautiful, with a birthmark on her face the shade of wine in a glass.

Unsuccessful, he'd stay, drink, widen his search. A mark on her arm the color of pencil lead? he'd ask. On her back, the shade of either New England brick or freshly mixed mortar? He poured liquids on himself, took bets what color it would dry. Cola dried the color of coffee. Coffee, cola-colored. Whiskey: the color of fresh cut maple, or fine sand from a virgin beach.

Winter came, the snow covering everything, wiping the city clean. He'd never seen so much snow, so much white. He spent most nights lying in the grass, the snow, trying to catch snowflakes in his mouth. It reminded him of going to the mountains with her, curling up in sleeping bags and watching the meteor showers. He could no longer remember which twin he'd dated, what her name was. The one with the birthmark.

He couldn't remember why he was in Wisconsin, so moved to Wyoming, thinking maybe that was where he'd meant to be all along. He decided he wanted to grow a mountain beard so shaved to start anew, then didn't touch a razor again. Nothing grew. In bars, drinking men asked why his arms were stained, why they looked like a child's collage. He answered with shrugged shoulders. Poured more drinks on his arms but didn't notice their reaction (cranberry juice: the color of freshly sliced grapefruit; cranberry and vodka: rolled off his skin like water off oil). He stopped going out, decided he wanted to learn how to ride horses, never went anywhere near a horse.

One night, July, he decided to start again. He couldn't remember the exact shade of her mark, only that it had tasted a little like a Bellini, sparkled. A girl at the bar: no birthmark but these freckles, up and down her arms, her cheeks. The color of the dots on the back of your eyelids after staring at the sun for too long. He sat on the stool next to her, said he wanted nothing to drink, no thank you. He asked her where she'd been and they talked all night about travels, constellations, beaches. Would you like to go? she asked. We should drive out to the elementary school. We can climb up onto the roof, watch the sky. There aren't any lights, just complete blackness. He looked at her and wanted to lick her arms, wrist to shoulder. Wanted to light her freckles like candles on a birthday cake and feel them singe his tongue. Wanted to strip and for her to see his body as a map. Wanted to fold into an origami version of himself for her, wanted her to point to the marks on his body, place dot stickers or pins, say, I've been there, and there. Yes, he said. Of course.

ON BRING-YOUR-KID-TO-WORK DAY, he stared at his computer, his cubicle walls. He thought of going to work with his dad when little—on days off from school or special occasions when his parents would write him a note. They'd drive me around the city, father introducing son to everyone he knew and worked with. Some days, they had to go to the dump and those trips were his favorite—watching the truck bed lift as he pushed a button, helping sweep out what didn't dump. The big hills of trash that seemed like magic. Now, he doesn't travel, doesn't even get up and walk around much. There's nothing magical like the dump.

WATCH THE BIRDS. Close your eyes, teach yourself to move as you've watched the birds move. Learn through imagined mimicry, sympathetic movement, mirrored imitation. Watch the eagle swoop down for the salmon, the hawk for the rodent. Their vertical plummet, headfirst, wings tucked. Consider the implications of terminal velocity. Look over the edge, count to three, jump. Be a bird. Tuck. Point head down, release all thought, enjoy. Your horns will catch you.

CHRISTMAS WOULD BE IN DECEMBER. This was their novel idea, how everything had worked out. And, what the hell. They would descend on December like elves—like real, honest-to-God, excited elves—and take it over, make it their own. They'd celebrate the hell out of it.

At first, they'd had something to prove. They didn't say this to each other, or aloud at all. Saying it aloud wouldn't have proved anything, would only have suffocated any kind of point. If absolutely necessary, maybe in whispers to the backs of closets, sure no one else could hear or know.

They believed circles were stars and green was violet. They spit when meeting people and said "upside down" instead of "please." Tied their shoelaces with lashing knots and wore them on the wrong feet. And they celebrated Christmas in June.

When even June became too regular, too conventional, they started anew in January, celebrated Christmas a new month every year. They stopped wrapping their presents for one another. One year, they hid each other's presents out in the yard like Easter eggs. The next year, glued them all to the ceiling, upside-down-Christmas. They looked at one another, then up at the ceiling. Pointed, said, please?

Then it came full circle and was December's turn. They fretted. They worried they weren't proving any point. If you can't beat 'em, they said. Christmas! they said. Christmas in December! They did it up. Left out cookies and milk, then ate and drink half of everything and left crumbs behind. They tracked in snow boot prints. Decorated, sang carols, planned on going to Christmas Eve service.

Christmas morning, they handed each other their presents, ripped at wrapping paper, kept warm in the pajamas they'd exchanged the night before. They celebrated. Then, bunkered behind their opened presents, they looked at each other. What now? they asked. What now? And they didn't know. They didn't know what now, and didn't know how to admit that, whether or not they should.

HE WAS ELECTED speaker of the world somewhere around midnight.

But...I don't want it, he said. I asked that my nomination be retracted, he said.

The nominating committee looked at him silent and intent for a moment then nodded their heads, once in unison. Yes, they said. We remember. But we then voted to override your retraction.

I'm not old enough, he argued. I don't have the experience, the wisdom necessary.

Again, they paused, held his gaze. They pointed at the sign, *you must be this tall to be speaker of the world*, as if that was all the explanation needed. As if height had to do with age or experience and wisdom.

Still, the sign was there. They had a point.

I don't even speak the language, he continued to argue, but they replied, either: you don't need to; or: of course you do. It sounded like gibberish, or maybe they hadn't said anything at all. He'd already forgotten how or what they'd replied, but he knew what they'd meant and, again, they seemed to have a point.

He searched for what else to say, how else he might be able to convince them that they'd chosen and elected wrong, and he turned his gaze out the windows. The near-full moon cast a smudged-blue tint over the sky, everything felt like that: smudged. He stood and watched the clouds slowly push across the night and forgot for a moment his appointment and then, once remembered, realized why they'd chosen him. They thought he could talk to the clouds, or could control them, or perhaps both, the ways he watched them so often and with such focus. They'd never said as much, but he could tell. He could see it in their eyes, and in the ways they watched him and would follow his stares up into the sky. He'd known this all along, though without realizing it until that very moment.

And if something should happen to me, he asked, finally leaving the clouds to themselves and returning his attention back inside. To the smudged darkness of the room.

What do you mean, they asked.

If I become ill, he said. Worst case, I pass away, or maybe something happens that we haven't even thought of yet. Something debilitating. Is there some kind of vice speaker of the world? What might happen until a new election, who would speak to and for the world then?

They looked at him puzzled, then conferred for a moment. While waiting, he again peeked outside and noticed the clouds were gone. And the sky looked empty, like he'd never seen it. Like coming to the end of the world and finding out it was flat after all, seeing it all just drop away. Like everything overhead had opened wide and swallowed itself. He wondered what the speaker of the world might say about that, how he would possibly explain this new absence of clouds, not a single blemish in the sky. Because he certainly wouldn't be able to.

WATCH THE SKY. Study it—the clouds, the sun, the moon, the vastness of overhead. Watch for patterns, predict what others would never recognize. Feel the forecast in your horns, learn to understand these feelings. Share with the others. Compare. Ridicule those who can't watch the sky, those who don't know better than to go out when it is raining. When the clouds have opened up, sliced and cut like gored by your horns, and released the spilled guts of rain, covering the earth in its intestines. Roar.

I WANT THE SKY to open up and empty itself on us, she said.

Thank God for the rain, help wash away the garbage and trash?

Taxi Driver, she said.

He loved that she knew the same things as he, wondered if the rain might wash that away with everything else.

Not exactly, she said. That isn't how I would have put it.

He looked around, horizontally, up toward the sky. It did appear a shift had occurred. Clouds were pulling in or pushing out. Something was happening, changing. You didn't bring your umbrella, he said.

I know, she said. Right. If I had, there'd be no point in wanting downpour.

WE HAVE THE HOUSE to ourselves, she said. And winked. Pointed at her eye and winked, exaggerated.

The kid was gone for the day. Out, with friends. They were left, alone.

They made for the bedroom, got out board games. Monopoly, Parcheesi, Scrabble. They couldn't find the dictionary; it was lost, given away, sold at a garage sale, invisible. They returned Scrabble to the closet. Boggle? No.

They watched movies, documentaries on TV, played video games. Had a slumber party in the middle of the day. Played cards. Every game they could think of, every game they could make up. Half-decks, two decks. They played solitaire, next to each other, watching.

They made for the kid's room, got out toys. Played dolls, dress-up, house. Made believe. Talked in stuffed-animal voices. Started projects, art, diaries.

Time was lost, running around without them, untethered. The kid called to let them know they were on their way back. They'd had fun, would be home soon. Time returned, retethered. They put away the board games, cards, dolls. Threw away half-finished drawings, diaries with secrets.

The sound of a car in the driveway. He ruffled his hair, pulled half his shirt out of his pants. She grabbed two handfuls of blouse and made fists, twisted. Drew the back of her hand across lips.

A car pulled into the driveway. Thank you so much, they said.

Oh, no problem. She was wonderful. We had fun.

He tucked his shirt back in. She ironed her blouse with the flat of her hand. They re-kempt.

Good, good, they said. Thank you, again, so much.

IN THE PARKING LOT, asked, he answered.

He thought of circumstances for which he'd tried to teach himself to think ahead: chess, SCRABBLE, pool.

From driver's ed, he remembers learning an acronym for changing lanes, but not the letters nor words. He only remembers the first trick: to look ahead, down the road, out beyond what is directly in front of you.

Later, parked again, elsewhere, a conversation about uncertainty, unrelated. He thought of chewing gum and walking, patting his head and rubbing his belly. He remembered someone telling him great chess players could think 15 moves ahead, someone else saying that just isn't true. Thinking too far ahead is a waste of time, the information unknown.

THEY'D BEEN WAITING for months for the clouds to part, the sun to make its appearance. Months that felt like years, a collection of years. Spring in name only, Winter had stayed longer than they'd planned or expected, the houseguest that wouldn't leave. They were worn out, depressed, had turned against one another, all while waiting for longer days and an energizing warmth on their skin.

And then one day the sky opened up, shook itself clean like a dog. Everything seemed too big, too infinite, like the first time he'd seen the ocean and hadn't known what to think. He couldn't comprehend the scope, the appearance of forever. He wished, when they'd still been around, that he'd been able to grab the clouds out of the sky; pull off a chunk like cotton candy, keep a little piece for himself. He did that sometimes: kept things, put them in his pocket for later.

HOME, it felt good to be home. The comfortable indentations of their own bed, the relaxing hum of familiarity. They'd gone away for the weekend. *To save their relationship* was the extreme way to put it, how he put it. *For a fun weekend away*, she'd said.

He paid the house sitter, the daughter of a friend.

Thanks again, he said. He paced the living room. Something smells…funny, he said. He inhaled. Paced, inhaled again.

Cigarettes? she asked. You think she smoked inside?

They'd asked that she not have anyone over and not smoke in the house. She could help herself to the food.

That isn't it, he said. He kept pacing. By the door: it does smell a little like smoke over here, he said, but that isn't it. Paced, smelled, paced.

Something in the fridge? she called. She was in the bedroom, unloading the suitcases, making piles of clothes, clean and dirty.

He opened the fridge, took in a deep breath. That isn't it either, he said. Paced. The more he tried, the more it bothered him. It was worse here. No smell here. Here.

He felt like a kid playing hide and seek, hot and cold.

The flowers, maybe? she said.

On the counter was a vase full of sunflowers and something else, something he didn't know the name of. She'd bought them at the drugstore a week before, two maybe, and now they wilted, drooped over the edges, looking down at the counter, the ground. He put his nose close, smelled, pulled back.

That's it, he said. He coughed.

Yeah, they get like that, she said. I guess we should have thrown them out before leaving.

He put his nose close again, smelled again.

Their last day away, on their way to the car, they'd stopped at a corner, waiting for the walk signal. Sitting there was a man selling his paintings, beautiful paintings of mountainscapes, fields of wild flowers. They reminded him of hiking and camping through, of growing up.

These are great, he said.

Thanks, the man said. Never seen the mountains. Just pictures.

The man flipped through his paintings, showing them all off, pulling out favorites. He thought of jumping in freezing cold glacier water after a day of hiking; sleeping in a sandy bed by the river, watching a meteor shower overhead.

He pulled one out of the stack, held it up at arm's distance, considered.

As he got close, exchanged money for the painting, he got a whiff of the man. He smelled awful, like he'd soiled himself; recently or in old unwashed clothes, he wasn't sure. He tried not to make a visible face, tried not to let the man know he could smell him. Thanks, he said. This is great. I'm going to hang it in my office.

Smelling the dead flowers, he realized that was what they smelled like.

What are you doing? she asked.

Throwing these away, he said. He held the flowers and vase in front of him, arms outstretched, head turned.

Don't worry about it now, she said. Let's just get in bed.

He put the vase back, made his way to their bedroom.

All night, he dreamt of mountains, glaciers, rivers. He slept restlessly, in and out of sleep, though awake he only remembered the beauty of his dreams. He didn't understand his trouble sleeping. Morning, he awoke sweating through his shirt. He felt damp everywhere, sticky.

He got out of bed, pulled on his pants. He took

a deep morning breath, made a face. The smell had gotten worse, was spreading.

He grabbed the vase and flowers, more wilted, more brown, and carried the whole thing outside. Garbage day, the trash can was out in front of the yard. Walking across the yard, he felt the cold, wet grass on his flip-flopped feet. Dumping the flowers in the trash, the vase slipped, fell in. He considered pulling it out, left it there. He closed the top, took a deep breath, and could smell only the fresh morning. It felt good. He was ready for this day. In high school, his P.E. teacher started every Friday by looking around, calling: "It's a beautiful day to run!" Today was a beautiful day.

He stretched, took another deep breath, exhaled. He started walking down the road. At the end of their street, he looked either way, crossed the street and kept going. There were no mountains for miles in any direction, hundred of miles, states away, but still he could smell them in the air. The trees; the water; the light, clean air. He walked the length of their street, stopping at the main intersection. He watched the cars, the stoplights. He crossed, turned off the road, started walking through the trees. He was in the forest, a state park, mountains all around, birds chirping, wildlife everywhere, just out of sight. All morning, he kept walking.

GROW ANTLERS. Focus, visualize. Apply a balm or lotion to the base. Prepare for the added weight but be ready to adjust. It never happens or feels quite as you'd expect, nor all at once. Balancing can be tricky, like learning to walk all over again, for the first time. Be proud. Stand straight, or as straight as is possible. Knock them around a little, rough them up. Rub them on trees, the walls of your bedroom. Don't forget to be proud, exude pride. Feel at home, finally, as yourself.

IN SEATTLE, he highlighted, "Jesus wept."

In St. Louis, "For many are called, but few are chosen."

Somewhere in middle America, already forgotten, a medium-sized city in Ohio maybe, he found himself at a party where others were snorting coke off a table. It felt like a movie, like watching a dramatization. He tried not to think how early their flights might leave in the morning, how this was probably technically morning now. He tried not to stare, not to say, think, anything at all. Went back to his hotel room for the night and took pictures, cataloging the ways his room was like every other room. Tallied in his notebook: the painting above the headboard, a cottage; the carpet, green. He took the Bible out of the drawer in the nightstand next to the bed and highlighted, "Let them alone: they be blind leaders of the blind. And if the blind lead the blind, both shall fall into the ditch."

In college, he bought his textbooks used and, when given the option, always found the decision between marked and unmarked to be a difficult one. Did he want to follow the path of those before him, using their experiences as hints, study guides, or did he want the clean slate.

In Denver, he highlighted, "Man is born to trouble, as the sparks fly upward," believing himself to be guiding those who come after. Sometimes, he read until finding something fitting his place, physically, emotionally. Other times, he'd open and highlight randomly. When he stopped to think about it all, he thought of himself as Hansel or Gretel, leaving crumbs behind for others to follow his path. He was a missionary. He was Johnny Appleseed. He was trying to help travelers find their way to him, or maybe to God, or to he-didn't-know-what.

In Houston, he called an old roommate and made him try to guess where he was. What is the painting above the bed, the friend asked. The color of the walls? The carpet? He could hear in his voice he was getting close.

HAVE YOUR TOES always been like that? he asked.

Like what?

Like that. He motioned with his head, confused by the possibility that she really might not know what he meant. She looked at him, down at her feet, back at him. He was treading water, resting his arms on the pool edge, his legs kicking; his eyes watched her feet dangling from the lounge chair, where she'd been reading until he'd disrupted her.

Webbed there, between the two small toes.

Webbed?

What do you mean "webbed, question mark"? Yes, webbed. He pushed with his arms and kicked his legs, sat up on the edge where his arms had been. He reached out and grabbed her foot, I mean, they aren't amphibian or anything, but that's webbed.

"Not amphibian"? Thanks.

You know what I mean.

I don't. She grabbed her foot and pulled it into her. What are you talking about?

That. He pulled her foot back and spread her two smallest toes apart. That webbing. I'm not saying it's gross or anything, but that ain't normal.

It ain't? she asked, laughing. Your toes aren't like that? I never even noticed before. I guess I just figured that's how everyone's were.

He swung his legs up and out of the water and presented her with his foot as evidence.

Well. Why'd you even point it out? she asked, looking only barely convinced. Especially if it "ain't even gross or anything." She made air quotes with both hands and laughed again.

I don't know, I'd just never noticed before. And he was surprised he hadn't ever noticed before. Surprised no one else had either.

He pushed off into the water and swam to the other end of the pool, wondering if they helped her swim faster at all.

TRY TO LET IT HAPPEN NATURALLY. *Don't think about it, don't think about not thinking about it. It isn't in your shoulders like you think. The most common misperception. A whole generation, more, all doing it wrong, like a mistaken translation. Try to forget everything you know—not just regarding the action, but everything. This is the first step, though, admittedly, the hardest. Impossible for most. It is in the neck, the small of your back, your triceps. But if you haven't been able to forget everything, knowing this is pointless. Will only make it worse. If you think about where it is and isn't—the shoulders, the neck, the back, muscles in your arms you didn't know you could control—you'll never get it. But if you get this far. If you get it.*

SHE LOOKED OUT the window, said, We went bowling there.He looked at her. You won't ever go bowling with me, he said. You always say you're too embarrassed or whatever.

Well, we didn't really bowl. We got a lane but then just sat there and drank. We watched everyone else bowl and made fun of people. We talked.

A mile down the road, she pointed out the window again, at a Denny's. We ate there a couple times, she said. She pointed across the street at a big, strip-mall parking lot. And we parked there a couple times. We never really did anything, just sat in the car and talked. Listened to the radio.

He could picture her, sitting in the passenger seat. Putting her seat back, stretching her legs out across the dash, across his lap, taking a couple swigs from his flask or a bottle.

He knew this was a mistake, but couldn't help himself. Like in that movie he'd always wanted to watch together but she'd always picked something else—"You know how it is—you don't really want to know, but you just have to." So, he'd asked, and she'd said, *fine, you want to know. I'll do even better. Get in the car. I'll show you.* He didn't know why he was doing this to himself but he kept driving, getting the tour. He took notes, already planning alternate routes, ways to navigate this city without having to see those landmarks, having to think about it more than he already did.

HE TOOK A JOB as a mason, put his hands to work. Carried bricks—moving and stacking and breaking in half when needed. On breaks, he rubbed his hands into them, sawing with the sharp edges and corners and slapping with the long, flat sides. He let the mixer have at them like part of the cement. At home, after work, he never rinsed them clean, the mortar setting, soaking in, drying and cracking and turning his skin brittle. It melted in, the mortar, coursed through his hands like blood, and he began to feel new. He finally stopped thinking about what she'd said, that word.

He gave his hands paper cuts, rope burns, cigarette, and oven scars. He wanted to tear them apart, break them into as many pieces as they had bones, then again, before putting them back together like a puzzle.

He bought a weight bag and punched it until he bled, then, to help them heal, wrapped his hands in berry vines he'd pulled from the ground by the side of the road. The thorns needled his palms and the berry juices mixed with his blood; red trickled down his arms like spilled wine, dried like mortar.

Finished—after his fingers bent, if at all, in sharp and harsh angles; after knots raised and didn't heal; after scars grew permanent and indistinguishable from the natural folds; after embedded gravel grew to look like knuckles and knuckles looked like any other part of his hand—he looked at his hands and they finally looked like something that belonged to him.

He could no longer grab small objects—shoelaces, zippers, necklace clasps. He wished he could pick up a piece of paper and a pen, write a note, then fold the paper into what he'd always promised he'd show her how to make.

I STILL HAVEN'T cleaned my sheets, she said. She was turned so he couldn't see her face, but her voice sounded apologetic. Or maybe just drunk.

He looked and the blanket was kicked down to the foot of the bed, and it was true: over near the wall, the sheet still held the outline from his arm, backwards like a print. He remembered how she'd run her fingers over the raised skin and still-bright-and-shiny black of the fresh ink. And he remembered someone telling him that when you drink a lot, a new tattoo bleeds more.

She excused herself to the bathroom and he lay on the bed. Moved his arm around trying to match it to its twin. He thought of what he might get next. He already wanted that shininess again, another part of himself changed, something new.

HE OPENED HIS ARMS, spread them out in presentation, prepared for something with weight: a bag of cement, a box of books, a stack of lumber.

It seems repetitive, she said.

He pulled them back in to each other, slowly, readying for something smaller, lighter. A box of breakables, a blanket, a baby. He made note of the differences in weight.

Meaning? he asked, though knew.

I don't know. Too similar.

You said the last was your favorite.

She thought about that, nodded her head. Maybe you shouldn't do all these for me, she said.

Maybe, he said. Maybe not.

GET IN YOUR CAR, *drive. Options, all valid: alone, together, for yourself, for someone else. Look for: something specific, nothing at all; a job, a home, your past, some kind of meaning, something that never existed in the first place. Choose cities at random, avoid them. Argue. Blame the road, the weather, the Badlands—the prairie dogs, the buffalo, Wall Drug. The past, the lack of past. Mt. Rushmore, the price of gas, the Tetons, all the rain, the lack of rain. Choose more cities at random, avoid them also. Set out for the first city chosen and avoided. Admit defeat. If not yet possible, continue, repeat.*

I HAVE A SURPRISE FOR YOU, she said with his first step through the door from work. He looked around the apartment, smelled the air. Nothing looked or smelled like a surprise.

Don't think about it, she said. Follow me.

She grabbed his hand, fingers interlocking, led him back out the door, down the stairs to the car. Inside, she laid out her hand across the emergency break and he grabbed it again.

From the moment he first saw her, he had been fascinated by her fingers. He was attracted to her, in love with those fingers. Her hands were large and looked tough, like they could choke the life out of a dying animal, put it out of its misery if necessary; but also delicate, fragile. And the best part: a subtle but distinct marking, a raised stripe of skin between the first two knuckles on her index and middle fingers, right hand.

When I was little, she said. We were camping, and I was helping my dad cut wood for the fire. We were going to roast marshmallows. He was showing me how to swing the ax, I rested my hand where I shouldn't have, and the ax slipped. It chopped off my two fingers. It happened so fast, and I was so in shock, I didn't feel a thing. Just looked down and my fingers were gone, blood shooting everywhere. We piled into the car and drove to the nearest hospital as fast as we could.

And they were able to reattach them? he asked. He noticed himself thumbing the ring of skin between her knuckles. He'd never asked about them—though he'd marveled, he'd dreamt of them—unsure how to ask, if they were something she liked to talk about or preferred to avoid. An accident she tried to forget or something she was proud of. He looked closer at her fingers; the scars so much less than he ever would have imagined for a reattached body part.

No, she said. They weren't able to. I wore these large bandages for a long time, let them heal. My dad felt so horrible, couldn't ever get over the guilt. I told him every day it was OK, I knew it was just an accident, I loved him. Months later he left, moved to Alaska, I think, maybe.

But?

They grew back. Every time I took off the bandages, rewrapped them, the wound had closed a little more, the stub had grown a little longer. After almost a year, they'd completely grown back.

He remembered, when little, capturing worms in his back yard. He'd cut them in two with the Swiss Army knife he'd gotten for Christmas, watch the one worm become two. He remembered the summer vacation in Florida. Trying to catch anoles, grabbing them by the tail, watching as they ran away, tail still pinched between his fingers. His parents told him it was OK, their tails grew back.

I love them, he said, surprising himself more than her. He fingered the scars, twisting, circling. He kissed her fingers.

She held up her hand again, like she might be looking at a diamond in the sun, like holding a slide to the light. I've never really told anyone. I've always been curious why they grew back though, always wondered if it would happen again.

At the copy shop, she pulled him in, parked. The place was empty, a bored employee on the phone in the back looked up when they entered but didn't move to help. She kept pulling him, over to the side, to one of the self-help stations. She pulled a paper cutter to the edge of the table, opened up the blade. She put her hand down, pulling her fingers out of the way, leaving her ring finger laying across the line marking the blade's cut. Grab the handle, she said. She motioned down with her head, indicating a slicing down of the blade. You, she said. I want you to. He looked at her hand, the blade hovering above it like a guillotine, and realized what she meant, what she was asking. He looked at her other fingers, tucked under, out of the blade's way, stared at the scars he'd found so mysterious and wonderful. He looked again, one final time, at the blade's handle in his grip, at her hand underneath it, and sliced down, fast.

CUT FROM THE FRONT *of scalp back to the temple. Start where the tip of the widow's peak might be, if you had one, following the hairline. Make sure the blade is sharp to pull through the skin with ease, though be careful to not let it slip in too deep. Holding your forehead down with one hand, pull the skin above it back slow, like peeling the plastic off the top of a container. Tools that may help: tweezers, scalpel, any of a variety of dentistry instruments you may be able to acquire, the tip of the blade itself. Peeled back, the skin may stay on its own or you can hold it in place or, most recommended, pin it back with some kind of clamp, hair pin, binder clip, etc. Retrieve the small piece of metal or plastic or even paper that you've been keeping though you never knew why, and place it against the exposed area. You may need to move it around until in place; when there is a pang of regret or forgetting, you'll know how it fits. Fold the scalp back into place, reattaching as you best see fit. Don't worry about the scarring or healing, it will have already happened.*

HE WASN'T SURE what he was doing there—why she'd asked him to come; why he was standing in a motel parking lot, transferring a car's worth of a life into the dumpster—but she asked, so he was here.

This? he asked, holding up a nice set of silverware in a wooden box.

Garbage.

This? and he held up a big glass jar full of matchbooks. She nodded her head toward the dumpster. Garbage.

He stopped and considered everything he grabbed while she moved everything in armfuls, hand over hand. For every one thing he grabbed and held up and then threw away, she threw in three, four, seven things herself. He watched, counting these pieces of a life.

This? he asked, holding up a collection of ivory elephants. He tried to remember if he'd ever seen anything made of ivory before, outside of exhibits. His own grandmother might have had something, maybe. He couldn't remember for certain.

I don't think I'd want those even if I wanted everything else, she said. I think it would be weird.

Toss it all, she said, and he lifted them in his cupped hands, up over the dumpster's edge, and let go. But, in his right hand, between index and thumb finger, he pinched and held onto the smallest figure, brought it back up out of the dumpster and slid it into his pocket. He patted it on the outside of his pocket, then continued to throw out everything else, no longer stopping and asking, no longer caring about each individual item.

Later, the car empty except for a bottle of water and some cigarette butts in an ashtray she'd made in school as a Christmas present, the one thing she didn't throw out, he'd wonder if she kept it for sentimental or practical reasons. They'd go upstairs to their motel room and wash their hands and watch TV in a queen bed because that was the only room available. The phone might ring but they wouldn't answer it, and he'd want to ask something to try to start a conversation but wouldn't.

In the morning, filling up at the last gas station before the airport, she'd throw the tray away, ash and butts and all. They'd drive the last mile with the windows down to air out the smoke and the hot, dry desert air would be almost unbearable, harder to breathe than the smoke, but he wouldn't say anything. On the plane ride home, she'd fall asleep on his shoulder and not move the whole flight and he'd keep one hand in his pocket, fingering the elephant, rubbing thumb and index finger over every little curve, every ridge, memorizing it.

At home, after they'd retrieved their luggage and went their separate ways, he'd keep it, that tiny ivory elephant. He'd make a place for it on his mantle, or maybe toss it on the table next to his door, right next to his keys and loose change.

I WISH we'd danced more, he said.

More?

Or, you know, at all, I guess.

The series of songs on the jukebox had made him sad, nostalgic, reminded him of a scene from a TV show; real or imagined, he wasn't sure. Two teenagers dancing in a bedroom. He wanted to tell her all this, remind her of watching this show together. Remember when? But he thought she should maybe already know, or it wasn't worth saying.

We could dance now, she said.

I don't know. The setting is all wrong, timing off. It looks like it may start raining any minute.

We can dance in the rain, she said.

They looked at each other, he shrugged his shoulders. He fought everything, didn't know why.

I don't know, he said. I don't know. I guess I just wish we had. That would have been nice.

MAKE YOURSELF like a piece of paper: crease, fold corner to corner, half, quarter. Tuck piece A into newly-created slot B. Begin to recognize the replication of yourself. Pull tight like you barely, but perfectly, fit. Slide into yourself like a glove. Like a mitt. Remember the first baseman's glove you got as a present in fourth grade, though you'd wanted to play third base. How you'd worn that glove always, tried to make it a part of you. How your hand had been most comfortable under that mitt, something secured in its webbing: a baseball; your other hand, made into fist, clapping into it; collected and balled up paper. Wrap around yourself like that, like the baseball in the first baseman's mitt for the final out. Fold in tight and small, like a paper crane's origami heart.

AFTER, he followed her outside because she asked him to. And when he said something he shouldn't have and she asked why he was there at all, that's what he told her: because she'd asked. He sat and watched her smoke and thought she looked sad, or maybe regretful, or maybe neither and he was just reading too much into the way she inhaled and exhaled, the way she held the burning cigarette between her fingers and out to her side, her arm balanced on her leg. She didn't offer him one, not even a drag from hers, because he didn't smoke and he hadn't told her that now, sometimes, he did. He hadn't told her, but wished she'd offer anyway, wanting this moment to be one of his sometimes. Instead, when she wasn't watching, he breathed the smoke in deep, pulling it out of the air and into his lungs. He looked up expecting clouds and a wash of gray and black but instead found the sky splattered with stars, looking like a dark piece of paper with a million holes punched through and held to a light. He stared up into the sky and got lost in it, forgot where he was and why they were outside at all, and he wished he could open his mouth and consume everything overhead. He wished he could pull in the stars and the moon and the entire

sky above and swallow it, bite by bite, just as he had the
smoke still pluming out of her mouth as she looked off
into her own distance.

Aaron Burch has had stories appear in *New York Tyrant*, *Barrelhouse*, *Another Chicago Magazine*, and *Quick Fiction*, among others, and a limited edition chapbook, *How to Take Yourself Apart, How to Make Yourself Anew*, from PANK. He is the editor of the literary journal *Hobart*.